A Mermaid's TAIL

Written by Robin Lang

Illustrated by Monica Garofalo

ISBN: 978-1-954614-25-3 (hard cover)
978-1-954614-26-0 (soft cover)

Editing: Amy Ashby

Warren
publishing

Published by Warren Publishing
Charlotte, NC
www.warrenpublishing.net
Printed in the United States

I'd like to dedicate this book to all the children who dream of magic, wonder,
and joy. I grew up on a lake and I was always swimming. My mother would smile
and say, "You're going to turn into a fish." I would laugh and keep swimming.
For all the friends I made at my cottage, mermaids made us feel as if we were
flying through the water, helping the fish and any animals that might have needed it.
It was a simpler time then and we could truly let our imaginations be free.

Be those dreamers, little ones.

There once was a little speck of pink sand.
It was tiny, and cute, and ever so grand.

When the ocean was quiet, the little speck of sand could land,
and when the ocean was rolling, so was the sand.

The sun shined its rays way down deep
to illuminate a world ever so unique.

The fish, coral, plants, and sea life,
swayed in the waves by day and by night.

But there in the depths of the sea,
the colors were dull as could be.

And tried and tried as the sun might,
there never seemed to be enough light.

As the waves along the sand created a ripple,
that little speck of sand rolled till they were slow and simple.

Then, one day, the sun shined through the sea.
It saw that speck of sand and asked, "What could that be?"

It was unusual in color and shape,
perhaps a little awkward in the ocean's sea scape.

It tumbled along the ocean's vast floor,
as if it were searching for a little something more.

The beautiful bright sun rose high in the sky,
sending its rays through the ocean as if they could fly.

The warmth of the sun gave life to the ocean.
Along with the current, everything was in motion.

Next, a marvel the ocean unveiled:
that little speck of pink sand grew a tail!

Then a smile, and eyes, and arms as well!
And the sun's heart began to swell.

Now each time the sun faded and rose,
that little speck of pink sand would grow,

until one day—a sunny surprise!—
that little speck of pink sand opened her eyes!

She wasn't a speck of pink sand anymore,
but a mermaid sent to protect the ocean floor!

Then as she slowly swam through coral and kelp,
she noticed some darkness and knew she could help.

She swooshed her tail until everything started to glow.
The ocean came alive with color and texture, so …

As she swam faster, the ocean lit up.
She knew this was her destiny; she never gave up.

Then, each day with her majestic tail she would glide,
traveling the ocean's breadth far and wide

to watch over all her precious sea life.
This, she knew, was her humble delight.

And when bright days became quiet nights,
she would rest her tired blue eyes.

Forever grateful for the sun's brilliant rays,
she protected her ocean for all of her days.

Be happy, be well, and sleep tight.
Be grateful, little dreamers
... nighty-night!

CPSIA information can be obtained
at www.ICGtesting.com
Printed in the USA
LVHW071858220921
698495LV00002B/42

9 781954 614253